Dedicated to bees, and

My dad—who loved reading to the kids on his lap,

My children—who spent plenty of time on his lap and mine,

And Melvin, who thinks all laps belong to him.

Published by Melvin TC
PO Box 338
Schoolcraft, MI 49087

Photographs 1, 5, 6, 8, 12 and 13, in order of appearance, are © Zachary Huang; thank you Dr. Huang!

Thanks Lucas and Marshall Beachler, and R.D. Rivers for other photographs and so many other things...

Printed in the United States of America

ISBN 978-0-9915834-3-0

When I was little, I sat on my dad's knees.

Dad, a grown-up, was very tall.

I, a child, was very small.

My dad would read me stories.

My favorite was *Goldilocks and the Three Bears*,
because Dad would use different voices.

"Someone's been eating my porridge!" thundered Papa Bear.

"And someone's been eating my porridge," complained Mama Bear.

"And someone ate my porridge,"
pouted Baby Bear, "and it's all gone."

I could sit on my dad because he,
a grown-up, was very tall.

And I, a child, was very small.

On my dad's knees, we would read
and talk about lots of things.
He would answer my questions.

Now I am a grown-up,
and I still have lots of questions.

I wish I could sit on a bee's
knees, and ask questions.

But I, a grown-up, am very tall.

And she, a honey bee,
is very small.

If I could sit on a bee's knees, I would ask **"Why do you sting?"** 5

I only sting if you scare me. Like when I am getting crushed.

When I sting I die, so I really don't want to sting.

Unless we feel scared, we honey bees will mind our own business.

We'd like it if you say hello, and move slowly.

Please don't run or wave your arms. Bears do that when
they steal our honey and tear apart our home.
I might think you're a bear.

Stinging usually stops you and bears,
even though I, a honey bee, am very small.

And bears and humans are very tall.

8

If I could sit on a bee's knees,
I would ask **"How many bees are in a** hive**?"**

 There are about 50,000 of us in
the hive in the summer!

If we all stood on top of each other we
would be very, very tall … even though
we are very, very small.

We have three kinds of bees in the hive.

Most of us are female bees, the worker bees. We do most of the work, like gathering nectar, building honeycomb, and guarding the hive.

Male bees are called drones. They are bigger and wider than us. But still, compared to you humans, they are very small.

There is one queen bee. She is the only one who lays eggs that grow into worker bees. The queen is longer than all other bees. But still, compared to you, quite small.

Because you, a human, are very tall.

I would ask **"Do wasps and bumblebees live in your hive?"**

two honey bees and a wasp

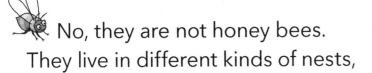 No, they are not honey bees.
They live in different kinds of nests,

bumblebee

sometimes on houses,

sometimes in trees,

sometimes in the ground.

They don't make honey for you. And they can sting lots of times before they die.

But still, bumblebees and wasps, like honey bees, are very small.

And you humans are very tall.

11

If I could sit on a bee's knees,
I would ask **"Where do you live?"**

Beekeepers keep us in hives, usually made of wood.
Hives come in many different shapes and colors.

We also live in the hollows of trees,
and sometimes in the walls of buildings,
but you humans don't like that.

When our home is overcrowded, we leave by swirling away in a cloud, called a swarm.

While finding a new home, we might cluster on your playset, or on a bush or tree.

We stay only a few hours or days.
We leave when we find a new home,
or when a beekeeper takes us away.

If I could sit on a bee's knees, I would ask
"What do you do in the winter?"

We make a ball around the queen to keep her warm. We slowly eat our honey.

We shiver to make heat.
Can you shiver?

We dream about
spring, and flowers,
and the warm sun.

15

"Why do you like flowers so much?" I'd ask the bee.

Flowers have nectar. We make honey out of nectar.

16

We carry nectar back to our hive in a special stomach.

There is a juice in that special stomach
that helps turn nectar into honey.

At the hive, I give the nectar
to another bee who carries
it in her special stomach to
the honeycomb.

The exchange, called
trophallaxis, actually occurs
from proboscis to proboscis
as shown in this photo.

Honeycomb is where we
store honey until we eat it.

It is one of our favorite foods,
and also one of yours.

Even though you humans are very tall.

And we honey bees are very small.

We also like flowers because they have pollen.

When we collect nectar, pollen gets on our furry legs. When we visit another flower, pollen goes with us and gets on that flower.

That is pollination.

Plants need to be pollinated so
they can make your favorite foods
like beans and berries … apples
and cherries …

and pumpkins. Even though next
to me, a pumpkin is very tall.

And I, a honey bee,
am very small.

If I were sitting on a bee's knees, I'd ask **"How do you find flowers?"**

We smell really well. When we find flowers, we tell the other bees where they are with a special dance, called the waggle dance.

Can you waggle?

We have four wings, but they overlap
and look like just two. Our wings make the
buzzing sound. Can you buzz?

We have six legs. Humans, with only two legs, are very tall.

But even with more legs we honey bees are very small.

All of our legs have knees … but you can't sit on my knees because you, a human, are very tall.

Perhaps I could sit on your knee instead, and be your friend.

"Like honey, that would be very sweet," I said to my new friend, the bee.

24

CPSIA information can be obtained at www.ICGtesting.com
Printed in the USA
BVOW07*1917030316

438974BV00003B/3/P